"Every night I lean against the weeping willow that touches the edge of the motor court." *Grace Notes* is a sharply-constructed book of matched edges of poems, prose poems, and collage. It is an elegant willow of a book that will reach into the depths of your motor court. *Grace Notes* is divine, but not like that. Meet the Literary Trinity: Poetry, Prose Poetry, and Collage. I worship this book.

–**Bill Yarrow**, author of ***Blasphemer*** *(Lit Fest, 2015)*

"Tomaloff and Tuite work in a wonderful discordant harmony that matches Higginbotham's artwork to perfection. Alone each contribution is full of wonder, but together they create a sense of awe."

–**Ryan W. Bradley**, author of ***Winterswim*** *(CCM, 2015)*

"Pay your dollars gladly for *Grace Notes,* a main attraction masquerading as a multimedia sideshow. The counterpoint between poets Meg Tuite and David Tomaloff is exquisitely capped by images by Keith Higginbotham, and it all lingers. Language and image here are familiar yet new, welcome to the oneiric brain. Read and look out, literally."

–**Larissa Shmailo**, author of ***Patient Women*** *(Blaze Vox, 2015).*

GRACE NOTES

Meg Tuite & David Tomaloff

Artwork by Keith Higginbotham

Contents

always

sky follows blue shadows clogged
with clouds poised like a photograph
when sisters and I would squint our eyes
waiting to breathe through gray scenes of
childhood stowed away in some old Chevy
truck bed of our mind glinting black and
white back at a luminous landscape expansive
as open blinds unafraid of a double rainbow
more vibrant than any fever could imagine

VINYL SIDING VOW SONG

a furnace rises through
a pair of nameless clouds.

we play pick up sticks,
build patterns of heatstroke

on the radiator—
there is no one at the door.

when the phone rings,
we build it a songbird.

we bury it in a rusty cage,
tape over the windows

of the best sandcastle
our tiny currency will allow.

crumbling foundation

a tornado whirls around early morning
toothbrushes stir coffee as face cream settles
in the kitty litter a boot cuddles curdled milk
in the refrigerator while unread books and
passive boyfriends stare up from the laundry
machine rigor mortis sets in on scorned toast
time is dazed by this person standing in her closet
as though everything has been lifted relocated
in the midst of pretending to breathe she is too
small for the crooked ledge of another day

KITCHEN QUARRY CELL BLOCK SONG

cold rocks and debris,
an elephant rattling with the wind

against the fence.
divers here say they don't expect

to find your clothes in the well.
I said you should take them

with you when you go.

the basement door is lit up
like so many teeth in the rays

of the morning-set sun.
I listen to the rhyme schemes

of wind chimes, broken fingers
attached to the places—

to the hordes of the hands
and bodies that I don't remember most.

I heard

a man died in his sleep. his wife woke up next to him.
he wasn't fidgeting, this man who had slept on the right
side of their bed for fifty-two years, his last ten dangled
brain tissue, heavy, glass ornaments from the family tree.
burned out colored bulbs, tangled tinsel throughout his
neurons. but once a year, like a holiday, lights would
flicker, suddenly blaze. the man smiled at daughters,
sons, called them by name. he wouldn't smack them
or shit his pants. he'd grab his wife, hold her hand
                    and sometimes ask her
                          to dance.

UNLISTENING DEVICE

how many reflections
does a river hold?

write your answer in braille
on the mouth of the dirty snow.

faces in branches
or faces, or vice versa—

owl as a glyph or an anagram.

I slipped my name
to a cluster of fireflies;

I called myself july, meaning

sometimes a lighthouse
is a better lighthouse in reverse.

known snares of mesmeric currents

skies are roiling pink and I'm starving rooms with
the absence of you and where is nowhere that used
to hollow out the eruptive hours of indecisive head
lights gouging track marks of someone else's existence
on sullen windows painted shut and migraines dulled
by bathroom mirrors still curled around the breath of
powdered speech where laced up urgency is as close as
a woman's lipstick fat as the shaded tip of some storm
winded clothes battling the strain of dust devils driven
by the soporific fossil of unrecorded gray wishes dazed
in placid rivers crying for some kid to sweep under
waves and grasp some shiny history while inside white
spiral tiles are counted sitting on a toilet dismissed and
prophetic memories passed over waiting to be ripped
from a waiter's pad squeezed between two frightful
human tragedies of starched silence uncovered and
strewn from wreckage of need

GRACE NOTES AND PARKING RAMPS

cars were parked up and down the street
leading a dull and/or motionless parade—

the caller ID mentioned fire.

operator, my skinny ties have all left me,
but I remember their hands like flags.

we are getting nearer.

people stared as the waiter spoke to me.
his voice was wrapped in newspaper but

the newspaper was made of history books
in a language no one was meant to understand.

if you place your missing days on a calendar,
cosmo says your next orgasm should last

anywhere from three months to a year.

I am walking beside me

a day appears to happen   weather is reported
and some man finds a conscience while a grocery list
blinks on the counter in capital letters no cheese no
bread sit on shelves wondering what kind of cough
magnifies the need for another afternoon on the couch
when things have generated movement though not from
inside through the lick of evening a father is absent as a
match cannot find its candle and a cemetery caws the
sound of wind chimes while the warm sound of a mother
            reading stories recognizes its own past

NO CODE

blood on the invoice
cancels out my water sign;

the generosity marks
on my wrists and abdomen

scar over like we mean it.

every time a bird sings,
a man coins a contradiction.

I know songs that only
the worst of birds have known.

a banner reading *hallelujah*
crosses over the fjord—

radio cessna music—

no rescue undertaken
nor postcard ever returned.

five dollars to enter the craft show of my psyche

the stench of Nebraska enamels me to its flesh
of corn and leaking gas tanks rising over St. John's
motor court empty bottles of grain alcohol scatter
memory over weed patches of my body disrobing
your face inching into madness and corn creeps
waving at all the places I'll never go after I get five
bucks for a potholder I crocheted a lady all hopped
up on eruptive lack of generosity when it cost one
dollar and I shrugged when she waited for what sky
is yellow-knobbed as passive and oddly immune to
activity every night I lean against the weeping willow
that touches the edge of the motor court and watch
for the outline of someone scratching the left side of
    his face leaning into a wind that doesn't exist

BETWEEN YOU, JOHN DEER, AND THE MOON

we held a séance the night of the big game.

elephants and small-time senators—
lions snaking the heartland between

rusted aluminum and poorly laid sod.

I knew a man once who was so deaf
he couldn't hear himself sneeze.

and you were there in the dream,
but you were a song someone remembered,

a war dirge echoed by straw men
whose only remaining line intoned

something's pretty got to come out
of this mess in the morning you would think.

collisions without diversion

skin moist with the groin of the city
capable of anything caustic as an insurance
agent who sticks a penknife inside the gut of
paper stacks and fills the holes with plaster
he bought from a sales clerk at Home Depot
who dug a well one night with his buddies
and a backhoe in stagnant suburbia to keep
water bills from permeating sweat   lacing
his rank polyester t-shirt while purple
veins trace strange white-capped ranges
of a woman's legs stark and frightened as
fluorescent lights stalking out of red cuffed
shorts as she bites her cuticles and wonders
if *Frosted Pomegranate* or *January Garnet*
is the perfect shade for her bedroom walls
           mute and haunted by lack
              of saliva and flush

ON THE MECHANICS OF PORCELAIN

incidentally, freefalling
from the roof of a painted-on town,

I counted bricks because I'd learned
not to count the floors from this high up.

>   *your uncle,*
>   *the one*
>   *in the space program,*
>
>   *or that photo*
>   *of your*
>   *granddaughter on a horse.*
>
>   *I'm thinking of them now,*
>   *though neither*
>   *of them was there.*

I had a problem with the spiders,
and then I relapsed, but now I'm good again.[1]

every time your sisters call,
I am sure the drapes are in need of repair.

>   *I am certain I believe in drapes.*

---

[1] "relapse" line owes a debt to Nicholas Ravnikar

full circle

brakes are set on my wheelchair by the window
of some triple-chin mountain reclining Hitchcock
movie I sneak down and shudder on the staircase
as birds beaks blood blast across the screen I push
my face against as our mow-the-lawn-every-Friday
neighbor Ed is lowered into a squad car in handcuffs
after his wife is found buried beneath a bank of lilies
wafting throughout the house when I still think mom
is coming home from the hospital listening to dad's
speech on baseball and Churchill over dinner peas
breathing in and out tripping to brother's Led Zeppelin
beat by a husband who keeps his fingernails sharp turn
as we snort angel dust three cars on the highway my
sister sucks in and hands me a joint of my hips replaced
with metal railings the nurse snaps shut my lips when
you say it's a snag in our marriage ripe with the bloom
of wedding photographs that freeze our faces happy
as the lady in white shoves me from side to side to
       secure my sagging diaper

TRANSOM NOTES
[bent light song]

the bricks still burning
in the pale of an abandoned nursery.

this is where we kept your father
is what the motion detector camera said,

as if they were the words
you most wanted to want to hear.

they make real songs from this—

a nametag plunges through
whipsawn branches,

so heavy a sound its fall,
it nearly woke me right in two.

stray

a man drove to animal shelters across
the county like other men drive to strip
clubs after mom and her two cats died
paid cash for all twenty pairs of eyes
that followed him while he paced hopped
up on Flonase and Animal Crackers
listened to his gnashing incisors arthritis
crackling through joints screaming sinuses
men get struck by lightning six times more
than women mounting the price of litter
to wear what to the grocery store and why
he never dated they howled like his mother
               but let him smoke inside

NAMED AFTER THE GREAT STATE BIRDS

do you remember that fountain where
you played as a child? well, it isn't there.

can you picture the way a mountain range
can fix itself across the horizon just so?
no one there could, even if they lied.

and we tied used tires to television sets,
piled them meticulously in the shapes
of people we admired.

a man with a lien on his mouth declared
there were rules to the universal code,

said the insects already knew them.
said he was talking now only to us.

he said the only rule in bridge
is that a gentleman never mentions it.
[he also said this isn't bridge]

you wouldn't believe the sparks
arcing off the pines—
their limbs dragging rubber-jacket wire
in a race against time that neither of them has.

the beating light of an undefined hour

she felt enchanted, life was an uncomplicated auction
until a visitor saw all her luck stampeding out the door
rusted horseshoes she'd found in the backyard hung
upside down she began to slouch again worried she
was impossible to climb calendars impregnated her
with white blank dates heavy with expectation strained
by frantic engagements she made up and penciled in
weight of things not done blew the gust of her into an
artifact deep cleavage rooted her eyebrows in chronic
disappointment as her hands grew older ghosts who
    opened and closed the past like Venetian blinds

VANITY FAIR VERSUS THE CHARITY HOT

on a day when another
of your famous birthdays arrives,

you are scraping mustard peels
gone bad from your crumbling facade.

you are not so much a building
but something akin
to the reverse action instead.

we chewed old gum from the boot heels
of priests when you
said it would get us closer to god.

we lit cessna engines ablaze,
and we took like arrow to sky—

we'd fashioned crosses
from the landing gear years ago.

at your party, we spoke with shadows
to nametags marked only as *coming* or *gone*.

eventually the band died
[ironically, they called themselves the saints]

weatherfish flew into my bed sheets all the morning long.

missing link

she spritzes ragged plant underarms
dusted by yawns weary with yellow-
paged skin drunk on recliners knick-
knacks a TV layering lethal lives no
body ever drudged in crooked a scar
as the cleft palate she blots with beige
make-up before unlatching the screen
door smiling as luminous as the bicycle
she never rides leaning against her
trailer when she only peeks out once
a day to check for clouds and if the man
separated by weeds and her unspoken
ledge of lust will notice her when he
    drags himself out of his truck

NOTHING MADE OF WATER

body parts go missing
in an ocean
of errant lakes—

the eyes of matryoshka
millipedes reflect

sitcom life giving way
to the blue glow

that trades nightly
in clock groans and sleep.

> [offstage: *the radio
> man is not your friend*]

an ogre of vultures has taken
residence on the patio set.

I wake in circles
to a state that
has never seen true sky.

unsheathed behind locked doors

my early morning pee is intruded upon
by the kinetic yet non-hallucinatory
blue violet spandex of mom's Gor-Tex
girdle shrieking from its hooks I feel
its deranged heart beat constrained
texture of accordion's wings without
the music it smells of ivory soap and
lack of dignity the facade breathing of
bound decay captive skin folding into
itself where no wind can touch density
of weight stretching the breasts up to
an elevated evening bath which must
be an amplified vacation for the boxed
in parts of my mother held hostage by
                    rabid elastic

OSLO [to which I have never been]

yet another of your
famous birthday parties

is a capsized wreck,
named for an undisclosed
anomaly of time.

I confess now that I have
never seen the sea.

      [you confess that
      you've known this]

I've sorted book
spines by the number

of letters common
to our family names.

I've measured raw thirst
by the cobwebs
that form across my teeth.

one day you just wake
and the rope that once

held you to the sky has been
replaced by a cheap chandelier.

my nurses are not Facebook friends

last night's martinis explode all
over my Facebook page wind
bruises puff up party dresses
with blush poinsettia's new
improved blood underscoring
hollow eyes that surface mirrors
not photos of me as a hot ice cream
sundae scooped into a blue and white
porcelain bowl whipped cream and a
cherry when it's a cold metal sandwich
of breast plastered between plates holding
its breath trying not to swallow one in ten
women who develop cancer from the goddamn
test balance mornings when the bed is a cloud
mass striated day ahead bandannas replace hair
while a daily mantra is embedded in dirt on my
back one white flower pushes up out of cracks
fake like someone stuck it there instead of
another round circle of women hooked up
to a port-a-cath drip six hours plugged
in to music and yes I've filled out endless
forms somebody files away but the martinis
            are my fucking business

THE HEIST [insomniac witness]

the stars were hand-loaded onto trucks
bearing no resemblance to the moon.

> [I don't count
> so well,
> or I don't count]

a splinter is the same as a whole tree,
should one position it right—

and no god would recognize you here,
sunk and simmered amidst so much snow.

> [I say I don't see
> so clearly;
> I keep watch for the silver coin]

> the perfect crime—

a whole night stolen, save the earliest
impetus of morning's unsuspecting light.

no sacrifice, no superhero

a dispatch of housecleaners
jump out of a red mini-van
my binoculars zoom in on
one greasy window as
houseplants mouth 911
dog Zoro two kids parents
all missing I don my cape
tuck my paper bag of live
crickets I feed my salamander
vaporize myself into invisibility
slink across the street
open the van door to two
dozen chirping insects
that cost two bus tokens and
my allowance now a dispersed
choir three rows in a mini-van
to keep this ring of intruders
from affronting my street
with their shoddy theatrics
of some clean-up team I'd
seen in every made-for-saps
movie-of-the-week Russian
spy flick where there's always
      a cost to vigilance

SNOW THEORY SONG

bring me the head
of the bottom of a river,

or show me on the doll
where the rain creeps in.

tie my face to the oars,
and make wing puppets

over the water
to calculate the direction

of the tides of snow.
we'll call it snow theory;

we'll make it look easy.
we'll sell it by the millions

on ebay, and we'll wake
in the morning with fresh

bills plastered to where
our eyes had been,

covered in the wear
of walls that won't

miss us when we're gone.

washing a dead body

start with a pink basin filled with lavender water
floating a washcloth while pillows are pulled out
from under arms between legs anywhere skin
touches skin how quickly a body moves from tissue
to stone morphine patches peel off bandages disclose
abrasions where blood seeps through pores hold
down eyelids until closed mouth is tougher can we
put dentures in asks the husband no everything
happens quickly lips are bridges hardened roads
bodies marred surfaces eyes oyster-shelled blood
pools deepen purple in splashes over extremities
yellow around gray teeth green-blue palette saturates
vertebrae like rings on a tree wash methodically softly
the exoskeleton of a molting dragonfly who no longer
feels sun-chewed nights ridden with terror the touch of
shaking fingers wash delicately for the family the lamp
glow undercurrent pulses through the carcass twitching
wings of the living who surround it

SIDENOTE [margin song]

our search party was greeted
by the bones of a mystery fair.

> [I cannot speak
> in the ways
> I would like now]

your grandfather referred
to the telephone cord as a noose.

you said, *but grand—*
things are not like that anymore.

you said, *we are all satellites now.*

quipped the old man,
or is it the other way around?

and no one from the bus line had
seen him. we found his duffle bag

near a decommissioned
phone booth off the military base.

we drove back the way we came—
denial bound for all that we have lost.

red krylon letters tag an underpass:

if you think nothing
never happens, they read,

it's because nothing never does.

acknowledgements

These poems have previously appeared
(or are scheduled to appear) in the following publications:

---

stray – *Right Hand Pointing*
known snares of mesmeric currents – The Radvocate
five dollars to enter the craft show of my psyche
– *A Bad Penny Review*
full circle – *Counterexample Poetics*
always – *Postcards, Poems & Prose*
unsheathed behind locked doors
– *Estuary: A Confluence of Art & Poetry*
GRACE NOTES AND PARKING RAMPS
– *Nauseated Drive*
VANITY FAIR VERSUS THE CHARITY HOT –
Nauseated Drive
OSLO [to which I have never been] – *Nauseated Drive*
SNOW THEORY SONG – *Nauseated Drive*

 **David Tomaloff** is an abolitionist vegan, pixel-herder, sound pusher, and maker of word-things whose works have been featured in network television shows, documentaries, independent films, and in fine literary outlets such as TheNewer York, Connotation Press, Sundog Lit, Lost in Thought, and A-Minor. He is co-author of the collaborative poetry collection YOU ARE JAGUAR (Artistically Declined Press). His latest chapbook, SLEEP, is available from Plain Wrap Press. Send him threats:

www.davidtomaloff.com

Meg Tuite is the author of two short story collections, Bound By Blue (2013) Sententia Books, Domestic Apparition (2011) San Francisco Bay Press, and three chapbooks.She won the Twin Antlers Collaborative Poetry award from Artistically Declined Press for her poetry collection, Bare Bulbs Swinging (2014) written with Heather Fowler and Michelle Reale. She teaches at Santa Fe Community College, is fiction editor for Santa Fe Literary Review, and runs a column at Connotation Press and JMWW.

www.megtuite.com

 **Keith Higginbotham** is the author of *Calibration* (Argotist), *Prosaic Suburban Commercial* (Eratio Editions), *Theme From Next Date* (Ten Pages Press), and *Carrying The Air on a Stick* (The Runaway Spoon Press). He teaches composition and literature, creative writing, and fiction at Midlands Technical College in Columbia, SC.

www.keithhigginbotham.tumblr.com

www.ingramcontent.com/pod-product-compliance
Lightning Source LLC
Chambersburg PA
CBHW040744250626
47164CB00006BA/168